Written for Marley, Jaxon, Kaden, Remani, Harrison, Oliver, Kirk and Tom

Poetry Park

Written by Leah Knight

Illustrated by Paula Nasmith

Would you like to hear about, an enchanting little park?

It's a place that's full of surprise, and magic after dark!

My name is Tom the park keeper, each night I lock those gates.

I jingle loudly with my keys, whilst beyond, adventure awaits!

I never wander very far. I wait, whistling my merry tune.

Only then do the creatures emerge. Excited by the sight of the moon!

Here's Marley, the

Magician, beneath a starry

sky of blue.

He taps his hat three times and cheers

NINKLE BINKLE OOODLE WOOO!

With a small crowd of nocturnal friends, the magic man can do no wrong.

He performs his greatest tricks; they've waited for all day long.

Ollie Owl calls from his post, to calm the excitement below 'Take
your seats, the time has come, to watch our favourite night-time
show!'

Above them all, stars are dancing. Animals gather large and small.

The magician feels a little nervous, as silence surrounds them all.

Marley makes circles with his magic wand; everyone knows what to do.

They're ready to rhyme, as he taps three times

NINKLE BINKLE OOODLE WOOO!

The audience are amazed! Harri squeals 'How did he do that?'

Excitement dazzling in their eyes, as Johnny Rabbit pops up from the hat!

'Dear animals of Poetry Park, I would like a volunteer

I need someone who is brave enough, to come join me up here!'

First Marley looks at Dala, 'I will not be part of this show!

I don't care for the spotlight you see; Leon I suggest you go'

'Thank you Dala for your kind request but I will have to decline

I'd prefer to keep my paws on soil, sorry, not me this time'

Marley knows these two are the best of friends, he chuckles and looks around.

Searching now, for someone else to make a willing sound.

At the very back a fox cub cries, bouncing on bright white feet

Please pick me, they all turn to see, him prance like popcorn in his seat

'Come along Jax, my dear boy, when you're ready, hop into this box.

Ladies and gentleman the time has come for the disappearance of
this fox!'

'Marley is the greatest Magician, no need to feel alarm

Retract your claws, clap those paws, this little one won't come to harm'

Marley makes circles with his magic wand; everyone knows what to do

They're ready to rhyme, he taps three times

NINKLE BINKLE OODLE WOOO!

Everyone gasps…….

Marley smiles before he demands silence,

it is time to bring him back

'After three, count with me,

1,2,3

loud and clear please,

JAAAAAAAAAAX!'

The fox cub jumps into Marley's arms, he has a carrot snack.

Tonight, the best of his entire life, he cannot wait to tell his pack.

I hope you had fun on the promenade, a place where dreams come true

Remember you can do anything you wish; we believe in you.

NINKLE BINKLE OOODLE WOO!

Goodnight

Tom (Poetry Park keeper)

Printed in Great Britain
by Amazon

64141982R00015